Party Poppers

Follow the Glitter Girls' latest adventures!
Collect the other fantastic books in the series:

Caroline Plaisted

Party Poppers

SCHOLASTIC

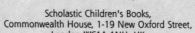

Scholastic Children's Books,
Commonwealth House, 1-19 New Oxford Street,
London WC1A 1NU, UK
a division of Scholastic Ltd

London ~ New York ~ Toronto ~ Sydney ~ Auckland
Mexico City ~ New Delhi ~ Hong Kong

Published by Scholastic Ltd, 2002

ISBN 0 439 99438 1

Typeset by Falcon Oast Graphic Art Ltd
Printed and bound in Great Britain by Cox & Wyman Ltd, Reading, Berks.

2 4 6 8 10 9 7 5 3 1

Chapter 1

"Hey, my favourite!" said Zoe, helping herself to a sandwich from the plate on the Fishers' kitchen table.

"Yes – I'm starving!" agreed Hannah, tucking in as well.

"Thanks Mrs Fisher," said Meg, her mouth already full.

It was Thursday afternoon, and the Glitter Girls had come home from school with Charly's mum. Now they were in Mrs Fisher's kitchen having some tea.

"So what are we going to do about this project?" Flo wondered aloud.

"What project is that?" asked Mrs Fisher as she carefully cut the crusts from some of the sandwiches to give to Charly's younger sister Lily.

"Well," said Meg, starting to explain. "Miss Stanley has asked us to find out about the town and the people who live here now and who lived here a long time ago."

"Miss Stanley divided the class up," said Flo. "And we've got to find out about life in the town in the twentieth century."

"And the other groups have to do the other centuries," explained Meg.

"Well, that sounds interesting," said Mrs Fisher.

"We've got four weeks to complete our project and we have to work as a group," said Hannah.

"I hope we can get everything done in four weeks," Meg said, being practical as usual.

"It sounds like ages!" Flo exclaimed.

"I know," agreed Zoe. "But Meg's right. I mean, we've got to go to the library and find out all the things that have happened here over the last hundred years before we can start writing or drawing anything."

"But I'm glad that we got the twentieth century, aren't you?" Hannah said.

"Yes," replied Flo. "We can get photographs and stuff, can't we? From that man in the market who has the bygones stall?"

"Good idea!" said Meg, grabbing a notebook from her school backpack and already starting to make one of her lists.

"And maybe we could find someone to talk to who's lived around here for years," suggested Charly. "Perhaps we could ask at the library?"

"Good idea!" Hannah smiled.

"I should think there are lots of people," Mrs Fisher said, sipping her mug of tea. "In fact, I think I know one of them."

"Who's that?" Meg asked.

"Mrs Greenfield's her name," Mrs Fisher said. "She lives in the home for the elderly that I visit every week. Lily really likes her, don't you darling?"

"Yes!" said Lily, her mouth now full of banana.

"So what's Mrs Greenfield like?" asked Zoe.

"Well, she's very old – ninety something," said Mrs Fisher. "She used to be one of the teachers at your school!"

"Never!" exclaimed Flo.

"You sound shocked!" laughed Mrs Fisher. "There's been a school on that site for more than a century you know!"

"Was the school rebuilt then?" Hannah asked.

"Well yes," Mrs Fisher said. "And Mrs Greenfield taught at the old school for years – all through the Second World War, I think. Eventually they had to build a new school – it was much bigger and had proper sports facilities and things. Mrs Greenfield retired about the time the building work started for the new school, I think. It must be over thirty years ago."

"So was the old school in exactly the same place as our school?" Charly asked her mum.

"Pretty much," said Mrs Fisher. "We just didn't have the same kind of playground and as much space as you lot do now."

"Did you go there?" Flo sounded surprised.

"Of course I did!" Mrs Fisher laughed. "I've lived around here all of my life. Mrs Greenfield was one of *my* teachers!"

"Cool!" said Meg. "I wonder how we can find out more about the school?"

"Well, why don't you ask Mrs Greenfield?" Mrs Fisher suggested.

"Do you think she would talk to us?" Zoe wondered.

"I'm sure she would," Mrs Fisher confirmed. "She's always got time for a chat. I could ask her, if you like. I'm going to visit her tomorrow while Lily's at playgroup."

"Would you Mrs Fisher?" Meg was sounding excited.

"Yes, it would be really cool to interview her for the project," agreed Charly. Charly was desperate to be a television presenter, and she was always looking for an opportunity to interview people!

"I'll ask her tomorrow and let you know what she says," said Mrs Fisher. "Now, have you all had enough to eat?"

"Yes thanks," said Hannah. "That was delish, Mrs Fisher!"

"I'm full up too!" agreed Zoe.

"And me," said the others.

"Come on, let's clear the table," suggested Meg. "Then we can get on with our project!"

The next day after school, the Glitter Girls raced to the gate to greet Mrs Fisher.

"So what did Mrs Greenfield say?" Charly asked, anxiously.

"She said she'd love to see you!" Mrs Fisher

smiled. "In fact, she's very interested to meet you because she's heard me talking about you and all the Glitter Girl adventures you have. And she wants to know all about the school – she hasn't been inside it now for about ten years."

"So when can we talk to her?" Zoe wanted to know.

"We've already told Miss Stanley about our idea and she thinks it sounds good," said Flo.

"Mrs Greenfield suggested you went to see her tomorrow afternoon at teatime," said Mrs Fisher, ushering the Glitter Girls into her car.

"We could make her a cake for tea!" Meg exclaimed excitedly.

"Cool!" agreed Hannah.

"Sounds like our project has begun," said Charly.

"Go Glitter!" everyone agreed at once!

Chapter 2

It was Saturday afternoon at last and the Glitter Girls were excitedly waiting outside Zoe's house for Zoe's mum to take them to visit Mrs Greenfield.

"I've got my notebook," said Meg, efficient as ever. "So we can make notes of the important things she might be able to tell us."

"Good idea!" Hannah said, hugging her friend.

All of the Glitter Girls were wearing their special denim jackets that Hannah's mum had embroidered with GG on the back.

As well as their jackets, the girls were wearing an assortment of their latest favourite clothes. Between them, they were a collection of crop

tops, bootleg jeans and mini skirts – all in vary-
ing shades of pink and purple!

"I've brought my camera too!" said Flo, showing her friends the fantastic purple camera that
she had been given for her last birthday.

"Cool!" said Zoe.

"We can interview Mrs Greenfield just like that
reporter from the local paper!" said Charly, feeling really excited about their latest adventure.
The Glitter Girls had been lucky enough to be
interviewed themselves a few times, so they
knew the kind of questions they needed to ask
today.

"Ready girls?" said Dr Baker, coming out of
her house. "Zoe, have you got that cake?"

Zoe proudly held up the cake that the Glitter
Girls had spent the morning baking and decor-
ating for Mrs Greenfield. It was a chocolate one
with frosted icing, and it was decorated with
Smarties. They'd all found it really hard to resist
eating it!

"Then let's get going!" said Dr Baker.

"Go Glitter!" they all cried, jumping into the back of Dr Baker's car.

★　♥　★　♥　★　♥　★

The home in which Mrs Greenfield lived was on the other side of town, but it didn't take them long to get there.

It was called The Beeches and it had obviously once been a big house before it had been converted into a residential home for the elderly. Dr Baker swung her car round in the drive and the Glitter Girls clambered out.

"Right," said Dr Baker, "let's go and find Mrs Greenfield."

They made their way through a big entrance lobby and headed for the reception desk. A smart lady dressed in a blue suit and a red shirt was sitting behind it.

"Hello," she said, smiling. "Have you come to visit someone?"

"Yes, we've come to see Mrs Greenfield," said Charly, pushing her pink glasses back up her nose. "We're the Glitter Girls."

"Oh yes, she's been expecting you," the lady said kindly. "She's in the Day Room – down the hall and second on the right."

"Well girls, have a good time," said Dr Baker. "I'll come back to get you in an hour's time, after I've done my shopping. Now, don't tire Mrs Greenfield out, will you?"

"No!" the Glitter Girls laughed.

"See you later, Mum!" said Zoe.

Charly, Zoe, Hannah, Meg and Flo made their way down the hall and gently knocked on the door of the Day Room.

"Hello?" they chorused, peering round the door.

Straight away, the Glitter Girls could see who Mrs Greenfield was. She was sitting in an armchair next to the window, and she was smiling at them, her eyes twinkling from behind her gold-rimmed spectacles.

"Mrs Greenfield?" Charly asked.

"You must be Charly!" said Mrs Greenfield in a gentle voice. "I recognize you from what your mother has told me. Come in girls! Come in!"

The Glitter Girls made their way over to the window eagerly.

"Hello, I'm Flo." Flo shook Mrs Greenfield's hand.

"How lovely to meet you, Flo. My sister was called Flo! And who are you?"

"I'm Hannah, Mrs Greenfield."

"And I'm Meg," said Meg, smiling.

"And I'm Zoe, Mrs Greenfield. We've brought you a cake for tea – we made it this morning!"

The Glitter Girls showed Mrs Greenfield the delicious chocolate cake and then placed it carefully on the table next to her.

"How lovely of you girls! Chocolate cake – my favourite!" Mrs Greenfield said. "But dear me, I haven't finished my tea from earlier. Shall I ring to get you girls some tea now? Or can you bear to wait until after we've had our chat?"

The Glitter Girls looked longingly at the cake and then at Mrs Greenfield. It was Meg that spoke for them all.

"It's OK, Mrs Greenfield," she said. "We'd like to have tea with you but we'd love to have a chat first."

"Oh, you are good girls," Mrs Greenfield said, sitting back in her chair. "Now you must stop calling me Mrs Greenfield. My name is Grace – hardly anyone calls me that now. But I think I'd like you to." Grace looked around the room. "Why don't you pull up some chairs and make yourselves comfortable and then we can have a chat."

The Glitter Girls each found a chair, and Meg took out her notebook and a pen.

"Now, what would you like to talk about?"

asked Grace, her eyes twinkling as she looked around at the girls.

Charly was the first to ask a question. "Mrs Greenfield – I mean, Grace – is it true that you used to be a teacher at our school?"

"Yes, that's right. I've lived in this area all my life. I even went to the school as a pupil, you know! The school that I went to when I was your age was called the National School. There were all ages of children from five up to fourteen. In those days, children left school at fourteen, you see. There were only two classrooms. The younger children went into one and the older ones used the other. There was a big fireplace in the wall that divided the two classrooms. My goodness it was cold in the winter!" Grace laughed.

"So who was your teacher?" Meg asked.

"There were two teachers in the school. The headteacher was Mr Spence. He was ever so strict and he used to sit at a special desk, high up at the front of the class. He taught the older children and his wife – she was lovely – taught the younger ones."

"Did you leave school at fourteen, Grace?" Hannah asked.

"Oh yes. Although I didn't want to!" Grace said, smiling at the memory. "Even though Mr Spence was so strict, I loved school and I just didn't want to leave. But I was very lucky because Mrs Spence asked me if I would come back and help out. It was the First World War, you see, and Mr Spence went to join the army. So I helped Mrs Spence at the school."

The Glitter Girls were fascinated by what Grace was telling them.

"By then there were a few more children in the area – children from some of the towns closer to London whose families thought it would be better for them to live here instead."

Grace looked at the Glitter Girls and then started talking again. "Mr Spence came back after the war and as there were lots more children, he asked me if I wanted to stay and train to become one of the proper teachers. Of course, I was thrilled!" Grace chuckled.

"So how long did you teach there?" Flo asked.

"Well, let me see . . . I suppose I worked at the school from when I was fourteen until I retired at sixty!"

"Cool!" Meg said, and Grace laughed.

"That means you were a teacher for forty-six years!" Charly said. "Wow!"

"I suppose I was!" said Grace, smiling. "And when I retired, I still came back and helped with reading and took classes when the other teachers were ill."

"How long ago did you retire?" Zoe asked.

"Nearly forty years ago exactly!" replied Grace.

Hannah gasped. "If you've been retired for nearly forty years then that means you are almost a hundred!"

"That's right," said Grace. "I'm going to be

one hundred years old next month."

"That's incredible!" exclaimed Flo.

"I can't believe it!" said Zoe.

"So you must know loads of people in the town," said Charly.

"And you must have seen some big changes," added Hannah.

"I certainly have," Grace nodded. "Is that what you wanted to talk to me about?"

"Yes," said Meg, and she explained to Grace about their school project.

The Glitter Girls sat chatting with Grace for a long time about lots of things in their town. From the railway station closing down and then opening up only a few years ago as a museum, to the day the first set of traffic lights arrived!

"I still can't believe that you're going to be a hundred years old!" said Hannah.

"Do you know," said Grace, "sometimes I can't either!" Then she laughed.

"Fancy having a hundred birthday parties!" Charly gasped.

Grace laughed. "Golly – I haven't had a party every year," she said. "In fact it's been years since I've had a birthday party – I can't even remember when the last one was!"

"That's really sad!" Zoe said.

"Well, my sister died several years ago and my husband Frank . . . he was killed in the Second World War. . ." Grace looked sadly out of the window. "So there aren't really any other relatives to give me a party, you see."

"What a shame," said Charly.

"Yes," agreed Flo.

The Glitter Girls jumped as they were interrupted by a knock on the door.

"Hello?" It was Dr Baker.

Zoe looked at her watch and was astonished to see that their hour with Grace was already up.

"But we haven't had the cake!" she exclaimed.

Dr Baker laughed. "Well you must have been

having a good time! Hello Mrs Greenfield, I hope these girls haven't exhausted you. I'm Dr Baker." She shook Grace's hand.

"Do call me Grace," said Grace, smiling. "And no, they haven't bothered me at all. It's been a pleasure talking to them. I hope I've been able to help you girls?"

"You have, but there's so much more we'd like to talk to you about," Flo said.

"Yes – like what happened to the school during the Second World War," Charly explained. "And what my mum was like when she was a girl!"

"Well perhaps you could come and see me another day?" Grace suggested. "Then you could share the cake with me."

The Glitter Girls looked down at it. Even without the temptation of the cake, they were keen to come back to see Grace.

"Can we come one day next week, after school?" Meg asked.

"Yes, we could come on Monday!" suggested Hannah.

Dr Baker laughed. "Do you think you could cope with seeing this lot again, Grace?"

"I'd love to!" she smiled.

"Go Glitter!" the girls all said at once, making Grace laugh.

"I'll see you on Monday afternoon! And I'll ask one of the carers if she can find a safe place for our cake until then," Grace said. "Oh, and Go Glitter!" Grace smiled, and raised her arm gently in the air, just like the Glitter Girls had done.

Chapter 3

The Glitter Girls chatted all the way home in Dr Baker's car.

"Isn't Grace nice?" said Hannah.

"Yes – and she seems to know loads about what's happened in the town during the last century, doesn't she?" replied Meg.

"You'll never guess, Mum," said Zoe, leaning forward in her seat to make sure that she could be heard by Dr Baker.

"What's that love?" Dr Baker asked.

"Grace is going to be a hundred in four weeks' time!" explained Zoe.

"A hundred?" Dr Baker raised her eyebrows in surprise. "Well, my goodness . . . no wonder she knows so much about the town. She's lived here for almost the whole of the last century! Is she going to have a party?"

"No," Flo said. "It's really sad. She hasn't got any relatives left to give her one."

"But what a shame that Grace isn't going to have a party for such a special birthday," Dr Baker said.

"It is, isn't it?" agreed Zoe.

"But who says she can't have one?" said Meg.

"What do you mean? asked Flo.

"Well, just because she *thinks* she isn't going to have a party, doesn't mean she can't have one, does it?" Meg said, with one of her knowing smiles.

"Oh, I get it!" said Zoe.

"Get what?" Flo asked, sticking her thumb in her mouth like she always did when she was tired or thinking hard.

Suddenly Hannah realized what Meg was getting at as well. "We could arrange a party!"

"For Grace!" Flo said, quickly taking her

thumb out of her mouth.

"Yes!" said Meg, excitedly. "I'm sure we could organize it, couldn't we?"

"Yes – we could have it at The Beeches!" said Zoe.

"Looks like we've got a double project on our hands, then, doesn't it?" Charly grinned.

"Go Glitter!" all her friends agreed!

On Sunday afternoon, Hannah was sitting in her bedroom when she heard a "RAT tat tat!" on her door. It was the Glitter Girls' secret knock!

"Who's there?" Hannah asked. As if she had to!

"GG!" came the password. Hannah immediately opened the door and the other Glitter Girls piled into her room.

"Hey, cool curtains!" said Zoe, looking admiringly over at the window.

Hannah's mum had just made them. They were made of a purple gossamer fabric that was shot through with pink silvery stripes – Hannah was really pleased with them.

"Thanks," said Hannah, grinning. "They're great aren't they?"

"They're wicked," agreed Meg.

The Glitter Girls had all begged their parents to decorate their bedrooms the same glittery shade of pink. Hannah's mum, who was a costume designer, was always making extra bits and pieces for Hannah's room. She had a beautiful bedspread made out of a patchwork of pink, purple and silver fabrics, and lots of big cushions that were decorated with beads and tassles.

"Anyone peckish?" said Flo, handing round a tin of Chinese fortune cookies. "I baked these with my dad this morning."

"Thanks!" said her friends, tucking into the cookies and settling down on the floor cushions. Meg took out a pink pad and a purple pen from her pocket.

"So," said Meg. "What are we going to do about Grace's party?"

"Well, my mum said that we probably ought to have a word with the lady that runs The Beeches to see if it's OK for Grace to have a party first," said Zoe.

Meg busily wrote this down on her pad.

"Perhaps we could do that tomorrow, when we go to see Grace," Charly suggested.

"Good idea," said Meg. "Now, what else do we need to think about? What kind of party do you think Grace would like?"

"Well, I shouldn't think Grace would want a disco party like us, would she?" said Flo.

"No – but we'll need to have food and drink," said Hannah.

"And some kind of music too," added Zoe.

"We need to make sure there's an extra-special party atmosphere," said Charly.

"Exactly," agreed Flo. "And I was thinking, if Grace taught for such a long time at our school, then there might be some people who still live nearby who were taught by her!"

"Yes!" exclaimed Hannah. "There must be! We could track them down and invite them to the party!"

"But how are we going to do that?" asked Charly.

"We could see if school's got a record of old pupils," suggested Meg.

"Hey," said Flo, "why don't we ask that lady at the local paper to put something in the paper for us? You know – asking people to come forward and help?"

"Nice one!" said Zoe. "I think that would be a great start! And those people could help us with our school project at the same time!"

"Yes, we musn't forget that we've got to do our project for Miss Stanley," said Meg. "We can't just do a party for Grace."

"Meg's right," agreed Charly.

"But can't we make the party one of the main

parts of our project?" asked Hannah. "If we get all these people involved, as well as Grace, then we're well on our way to finding out about all the changes that have happened over the last one hundred years, aren't we?"

"Sounds like a good idea to me," said Flo.

"Me too," agreed Zoe.

"I reckon we should check it out with Miss Stanley first though," said Meg. "We'd better make sure before we get going."

"Well, if she says yes, what else do we need to organize?" asked Charly.

"Well," said Meg, consulting her list. "If she says it's OK to do the project this way, the first thing we need to do is speak to the lady who runs The Beeches. And if she says we can organize a party for Grace, I think the next thing to do is contact the reporter at the paper to get her help in tracking down some of Grace's old pupils. And once that's underway, we can get on and organize the best hundredth birthday party ever!"

"Brilliant!" said Flo.

"Fantastic!" said Charly.

"Cool!" said Hannah and Meg together.

"Looks like the project could really be on then!" said Zoe.

"Go Glitter!" they all cheered at once!

Chapter 4

It was Monday morning and the Glitter Girls had arrived especially early at school so they could tell Miss Stanley all about their visit with Grace and the ideas they had about their project and Grace's birthday.

". . .so you see, Miss Stanley," explained Meg, "we thought we could find out all about things that have gone on in the town while we organize Grace's party."

Miss Stanley smiled at Charly, Meg, Hannah, Flo and Zoe. "I might have guessed that you girls would get up to something like this."

"So, is it OK then?" Zoe asked.

"Well, it's certainly a good idea. . ." Miss Stanley paused and the Glitter Girls exchanged looks.

Was she going to say no? But then Miss Stanley smiled at the girls again and carried on talking. "I think it might be a good idea for you to check with The Beeches first. See if the staff think Grace is up to a party – after all, she is quite elderly."

"We'd already planned to do that after school today!" enthused Flo.

"Good," said Miss Stanley. "And if they say yes, then you can start making party plans!"

"That's great, Miss Stanley!" said Flo.

The Glitter Girls hugged each other excitedly.

Miss Stanley smiled at the girls. "I wonder as well. . ." The girls' teacher looked thoughtful.

"What's that, Miss?" asked Zoe.

"You know that the mayoress is one of the school governors?" said Miss Stanley. "Well, when she was a little girl, she also came to this school."

"So she might have been taught by Grace too!" Meg exclaimed.

"I think so," agreed Miss Stanley. "And I'm sure

she'd love to be involved in the celebrations."

"Wicked!" said Charly. "We need to arrange to see the mayoress then."

"That sounds like a good idea," Miss Stanley said. "But don't forget girls, the main project is meant to be finding out about the town over the last hundred years. You must do your work for that."

"Course we will, Miss Stanley!" said Meg.

"Well, I look forward to finding out how you get on then!" Miss Stanley smiled once more.

"Go Glitter!" they all yelled at once.

★ ♥ ★ ♥ ★ ♥ ★

Charly's mum picked up the Glitter Girls from school that afternoon and took them all to The Beeches as planned.

"I'll wait in the garden with Lily," said Mrs Fisher. "Don't be too long, will you?"

"OK!" said Charly.

As the girls rushed into the home they

bumped straight into Mrs Billingham, the lady who managed The Beeches.

"Hello girls – have you come to see Grace?" she asked.

The Glitter Girls nodded. Then they explained enthusiastically about their plans and asked if it would be OK for Grace to have a birthday party.

"I think it would be a lovely idea, girls," she agreed. "We could hold it on the 24th – that's her actual birthday."

"Go Glitter!" the girls cried happily.

"Well – we'll talk about the details another day – we could probably have it in the dining room," said Mrs Billingham. "But in the meantime, I think Grace is waiting to see you with some rather delicious chocolate cake!"

"Hello girls!" Grace greeted them with a smile.

"Hi Grace," the girls chorused, as they each pulled up a chair.

"Thanks for seeing us again," Charly said, pushing her pink glasses up her nose.

"Help yourselves to cake," said Grace.

"Thanks!" they all said at once, eagerly tucking in.

"And here's some for you," said Zoe, handing Grace a plate.

"Oh, thank you," Grace replied.

"Grace, can you tell us some more about the changes to the town over the last hundred years?" Zoe enquired.

"Well, there are so many. . ." Grace looked wistfully out of the window. "I've been thinking about it since I last saw you."

Grace told the girls about the building of the new school, the one that they went to, and how it was built next to the old one, in the playground.

"Of course, the new playground – the one you've got – was built on the site of the old bus depot," explained Grace.

"Bus depot?" Flo queried.

"Yes – all the buses used to stop there in those days. Then they moved the bus depot to where the cinema used to be," Grace continued.

"There was a cinema?" questioned Meg.

"Yes," said Grace. "Everyone used to go to the Picture Palace. We didn't have videos and things in those days. And not many people had a television until the Queen's Coronation."

"Wow!" said Charly.

Grace went on to tell the girls about the Leisure Centre being built, the war memorial that was erected after the Second World War, and the time the town flooded.

Meg wrote everything down in her notebook, so the Glitter Girls could follow it all up later. After half an hour's talking, Grace leant back in her armchair and stifled a yawn.

"Well girls," said Mrs Fisher, who had appeared in the doorway with Lily. "I think it's time that we went home for our tea and left Grace in peace."

"Yes, thank you Grace," said Hannah.

"Thanks!" said Charly and Zoe, as they both stood up.

"Can we come and see you again?" Meg asked.

"Please?" pleaded Flo.

"Of course!" Grace smiled warmly at the girls. "You know, I've just had a thought. Why don't you go and see the mayoress? She'll know where all the town records are kept. They're probably in the Town Hall or the library – and there may even be some old photographs of the school and the town."

"That's a brilliant idea!" exclaimed Meg, giving the others a knowing look.

"Fab!" winked Charly.

Grace laughed. "I'm only pleased I can still help with a school project after all these years! Go Glitter!" she smiled.

"Go Glitter!" the Glitter Girls enthusiastically replied.

Chapter 5

Back at Charly's house, the Glitter Girls had a meeting.

"So," said Meg. "We've got the OK for the party on the 24th – now what do we need to organize for it?"

"I think we should sort out the guests first," suggested Flo.

"Good idea," said Zoe. "Let's go along to the newspaper office to ask them about putting something in the next issue of the paper. We could do that after school tomorrow."

"Great," said Meg, writing it down in her notebook. "But I can't come because it's my cello lesson."

"Neither can me and Charly," added Flo. "It's

our swimming lesson tomorrow."

"Oh!" said Zoe, feeling disappointed. "When can we go then?"

"I could go tomorrow," Hannah suggested. "Why don't we go?"

Hannah looked at the others, wondering if they would mind if she and Zoe went to the newspaper office on their own.

"Well," said Meg. "If we are going to get this party organized for Grace and the project stuff ready for Miss Stanley, we need to get cracking, don't we? We haven't got any time to lose! I reckon Zoe and Hannah should go, don't you?" Meg looked at Charly and Flo.

"OK," Flo replied.

"It's cool with me," said Charly.

"Great!" said Hannah.

"What else then?" asked Meg.

"We'll need party food," added Zoe. "Perhaps we could ask the guests to help out with that? You know, get them all to make something."

"And we'll need decorations," siad Charly.

"My mum could help us with those," suggested Hannah.

"And we need to arrange to see the mayoress," said Meg.

"How are we going to do that?" Hannah wondered.

"I know!" said Zoe. "Let's ask Mrs Wadhurst if she can call her and make an appointment for us!"

"Go Glitter!" everyone replied.

The next morning in the playground, Meg was bursting with news for her friends.

"Listen, I spoke to my dad on the phone last night and I was telling him all about Grace. He said that if the mayoress does know where some old photos and stuff are kept, then he'll be able to get them copied for us."

"That's a great idea!" exclaimed Flo. "I could

get Kim to help me mount and frame them. Then we could use them as a display for our project, couldn't we?"

"But wouldn't it be a nice idea to let Grace have some of the copies as well?" Charly asked.

"Charly's right," said Hannah. "Grace might be really interested to see them."

"Well, why don't we make a kind of mini album of the photos to give to Grace as well?" Flo suggested.

"Cool!" said Hannah.

"And we could write about how the town has changed in her lifetime too," said Charly excitedly.

"Yes," said Meg. "But are we going to have time to do a wall display *and* a book for Grace – as well as writing our project?"

"Meg's got a point," said Zoe. "After all, we've only got three weeks."

"Hmm," Flo kicked at some gravel as they waited to go in for class.

"Unless. . ." Zoe said thoughtfully. "Unless. . ."

"Unless what, Zoe?" Meg asked.

"Well, if these photos do exist, we could do a wall display, like Flo says. And if we track down lots of people in the town that Grace taught and stuff, well we could get them to write something about their memories of Grace – and perhaps let us have copies of photographs they might have as well. Then we could put it all together in a book for Grace. But if Miss Stanley will let us, we could show the book to her as our project book before we give it to Grace. Then we only have to do the one project, don't we?"

"That's a great idea!" said Charly.

"Do you think Miss Stanley will let us?" Meg wondered.

"Let's go and ask her now," Flo said. "She did ask us to let her know how we were getting on."

After lunch, the Glitter Girls were feeling very pleased with themselves. Miss Stanley had agreed that they could use Zoe's idea about the book and Flo's idea for the wall display as a means of displaying their project.

Meg pulled out her notebook and looked at her list of things that the Glitter Girls had to do.

"Right," Meg took the top off her pen. "Zoe and Hannah will go along to the newspaper after school today. Flo's going to organize the wall display and the rest of us will work on the book."

"I spoke to my mum about the decorations," said Hannah. "She suggested we could do bunting and stuff to go around the walls. And she thought they might have some special gold and silver balloons at the theatre that were left over from the Christmas pantomime."

"Great," said Meg. "We can have a decorations session one evening."

"Hey," said Zoe. "I wondered if we could

make a quilt for Grace?"

"A quilt?" Flo asked.

"Yes – my aunt in America told me about them once. They call them Friendship Quilts and they make them for special occasions."

"Sounds great," said Charly, "but when and how are we going to make one of those?"

"Looks like another thing to ask Mrs Giles about," suggested Meg, writing it down on her list.

"I'll have a word with Mum about it tonight," said Hannah, who was plaiting her long red hair as she spoke.

"It looks like we can give Grace a really fantastic party!" Hannah said.

Just then, the bell went. It was time to go back into school for the afternoon session.

"Come on – time for PE," said Flo. "We can meet up again afterwards."

★ ♥ ★ ♥ ★ ♥ ★

Later that afternoon, the Glitter Girls went to see Mrs Wadhurst. Meg explained about all the plans they had for Grace's birthday – and, of course, their project!

"So Grace – Mrs Greenfield – suggested that we went along to see Mrs Kirk, the mayoress," Meg finished.

"That sounds like a very good idea," agreed Mrs Wadhurst. "And she'd make a very good person to ask for help with your party, too!"

The girls smiled happily at each other.

"Why don't I phone the mayoress's office and see if I can arrange a time for you to go and see her? Maybe you could even have the party at the Town Hall – after all, not many people live to be one hundred, do they?" said Mrs Wadhurst, smiling.

"Please!" the girls all said at once.

"I'll call her this afternoon then!"

★ ♥ ★ ♥ ★ ♥ ★

After afternoon registration, Miss Stanley called the Glitter Girls up to her desk. "I've got a message for you from Mrs Wadhurst," she said excitedly. "The mayoress can see you straight after school today!"

"But only Hannah and Zoe are free this afternoon," said Meg with dismay. "And they've already planned to visit the newspaper office."

Miss Stanley looked at the Glitter Girls' troubled faces. "I'm sure Hannah and Zoe could squeeze in a trip to see the mayoress as well as a visit to the newspaper office, couldn't you, girls?"

Zoe and Hannah looked at each other and smiled. "Of course we can!" said Zoe. "You can count on us!"

"Go Glitter!"

Chapter 6

As soon as the bell went that afternoon, Hannah and Zoe raced to the school gates.

"Bye, you two!" Meg called, as she lugged her cello off to her lesson. "Good luck!"

"See you tomorrow!" Flo and Charly added as they set off to the Leisure Centre with Charly's mum for their swimming lesson.

Hannah and Zoe rushed over to Dr Baker, who was waiting outside the school gates.

"Hi Mum!" called Zoe.

"Hello girls!" said Dr Baker. "How are you two today?"

Excitedly Zoe explained about the extra trip to visit the mayoress at the Town Hall.

"Well," said Dr Baker, smiling. "It's a good job

I've parked up in the town car park. We can walk from here to the Town Hall and then perhaps I can do a couple of jobs while you two go to the newspaper office."

"Thanks, Dr Baker," Hannah smiled.

"Come on, let's get a move on," said Zoe. "It looks like it might rain!"

A short while later, Hannah and Zoe were waiting in the reception area of the Town Hall. They'd told the friendly man at the desk that they had an appointment to see the mayoress and they had been asked to wait for a moment.

"Hey – look at that," Zoe wandered over to a huge wooden board that hung on a wall alongside the very grand staircase.

"What does it say?" Hannah asked, going over to join her friend.

"It's the names of all the previous mayors and mayoresses of the town. Look, it goes right back to 1587! That's incredible! There's another one over there, look!" said Zoe.

Zoe and Hannah moved over to the other side of the staircase and started to read the second board.

"It's the names of all the people in the town that died during the First and Second World Wars," said Zoe. "We ought to include them in our project!"

"Good idea!" said Hannah. "Shall we write them down now?"

But before Zoe could answer, the girls were interrupted by a voice behind them.

"Hello – you must be Zoe and Hannah."

It was the mayoress. The two girls recognized her immediately from school assemblies and concerts.

"Hello Mrs Kirk," Zoe and Hannah said at once. "Thank you for seeing us."

"You're welcome," said the mayoress, smiling. "Come on in to my office and we'll have a chat."

The girls followed Mrs Kirk up the stairs and into a small but grand office. The walls were lined with framed portraits and photographs of men and women. Mrs Kirk could see Zoe and Hannah looking at them and explained that they were all previous mayors and mayoresses of the town.

"Now, what can I do for you today? I understand that you've come to tell me about a project you're doing for school."

"Yes, that's right," Zoe said, and she and Hannah took it in turns to explain to Mrs Kirk all about their history project for Miss Stanley and the ideas they had had about Grace Greenfield and her hundredth birthday.

"I remember Mrs Greenfield well – she taught me when I was at your school, you know." The mayoress smiled at the two girls. "I can't believe that she's going to be a hundred!"

"So do you think it would be possible for Grace to be given a party at the Town Hall to celebrate her birthday?" Hannah asked.

"We'd help to do all the arranging and stuff," Zoe offered. "We thought we could ask everyone who comes to bring some food."

"Well I think it would be an absolutely splendid idea!" Mrs Kirk said. "We could easily hold the party here. In fact, I think as it is such a special occasion, that the Town Council should provide all the party food!"

Zoe and Hannah beamed with delight.

"We're going to make a banner and some decorations," Zoe explained.

"And we're going to get some gold and silver balloons as well," said Hannah.

"Oh, and Mrs Fisher – that's Charly's mum – is going to help us to bake a special cake as well."

"It sounds like you're very organized," said Mrs Kirk. "What about the guests? Have you invited everyone?"

Zoe and Hannah explained that they were going along to the newspaper office afterwards to put an advert in the paper.

"That sounds like a great idea. I'm sure you'll get lots of people contacting you," said Mrs Kirk. "And I'm sure I can help spread the word in all the meetings I have to go to."

"We're doing a special presentation book for Grace, too," said Zoe.

"We're trying to find some old photographs of the town and the people who lived here," added Hannah.

"What great ideas you girls have had," Mrs Kirk said. "We must go and look at the town archives. We've got lots of photographs of the town over the last century. And there are the school records to look at as well. And perhaps the paper could ask people to send in some of their memories for the book?"

"Good idea!" said Zoe.

"Brilliant!" said Hannah.

"Now, you said that Grace's birthday is in three weeks' time?" asked Mrs Kirk.

"Yes, that's right," said Hannah.

"Well, I wonder if anyone has made sure that the Queen is going to send her a telegram for her birthday? The Queen sends them to everyone on their one hundredth birthday," Mrs Kirk explained. "It should happen automatically, but we don't want any mistakes, do we?"

"Can we do that?" Zoe's eyes sparkled with excitement at the thought of the Glitter Girls writing to the Queen and getting a letter back!

"I think that would be a terrific idea," said Mrs Kirk, who seemed to be as enthusiastic as the Glitter Girls were at the thought of celebrating Grace's special birthday. "Now, let's go and check the archives!"

Zoe and Hannah followed Mrs Kirk out of the room grinning at each other.

After a busy time with the mayoress, Dr Baker took Hannah and Zoe to the newspaper office, further along the high street.

"Hello there!" said a friendly-looking woman, as they walked into the office's reception area. It was the same reporter that the Glitter Girls had met when they had their Magical Makeovers stall at the school fête. "What can we do for you?" she asked.

Zoe and Hannah told her all about Grace and her party and how they needed to trace people who had lived in the town a long time and who also remembered Grace.

"That's a lovely story for the paper," the reporter said. "You say she lives at The Beeches?" She was writing everything down on her pad. "Well you came in the nick of time!" she looked at her watch. "I've only got thirty minutes to file any more copy before the paper goes to press!"

"Oh no!" Hannah and Zoe said, worried that they'd left it too late.

"Don't worry!" the reporter said, smiling. "I'll make sure that we get a good slot for this one!"

Chapter 7

At school the next morning, Charly, Zoe and Meg were eager for news.

"How did you two get on?" Meg asked.

"Well . . . Mrs Kirk says that Grace will be able to have her party in the Town Hall and that the Town Council will organize all the party food!" said Zoe, excitedly.

"Phew, that's a relief!" said Meg, smiling at the others. "What about the photos and things?"

"Oh, there were lots of them!" Hannah said. "Mrs Kirk introduced us to the curator who's in charge of the photos and he showed us loads. Photographs of the old school buildings and the teachers that Grace told us about. Including one of Grace with Mr and Mrs

Spence when she was a trainee teacher!"

"And there were some of the new school being built as well," added Zoe.

"And lots of photographs of the evacuees that were sent here for safety during the First and Second World Wars!" said Hannah.

"And there were some great pictures of the high street – it's really changed! There was a photo taken in 1912 and there was only one car in the whole street – and it was surrounded by lots of horses and carriages. And there was one taken in 1930 which had lots more cars and some telephone lines," Zoe said.

"And there was a brilliant one taken in 1977, – celebrating the Queen's Silver Jubilee. They had an enormous street party!" said Hannah, laughing.

"They sound perfect," said Meg. "Can we get some of them copied for our project?"

"We told Mrs Kirk about your dad and she said yes, once we'd chosen which ones we want, we should speak to the curator," explained Hannah.

"Brilliant," said Meg, relieved that there was some real action at last.

"And then we went to see the reporter at the newspaper," Hannah said.

"She remembered us!" said Zoe. "The story about Grace is going to be in the next issue of the paper!"

"Perfect!" said Meg.

"Oh, and we forgot to tell you about the Queen!" Hannah said.

"The Queen?" Charly asked, puzzled. "What's she got to do with it?"

"Well we've got to write to the Queen and ask her if she can make sure she sends a birthday telegram to Grace!" Zoe explained.

"Wow!" said Meg. "We ought to ask Miss Stanley if we can do that on school notepaper – Flo should write it because she's got the best handwriting."

"Then we can all sign it!" Flo added.

"Go Glitter!" they all yelled excitedly.

★　♥　★　♥　★　♥　★

That afternoon, the Glitter Girls all went over to Hannah's house for a meeting.

"So," said Meg, getting her pad out. "What's happening about the decorations?"

"Kim's helped me to do the lettering on the banner," Flo explained.

"We've just kept it to 'Happy Birthday Grace!'. But we'll need some help to paint the letters."

"No problem – we could do that at the weekend," said Charly.

"How about the quilt?" Meg asked.

"Well, I've spoken to Mum about it and she's thinking about how we can do it," replied Hannah.

"We'll have to get on with it soon," said Flo. "Otherwise we'll run out of time."

"So the balloons are sorted?" Meg wondered, ticking things off her list.

Hannah nodded.

"Oh and my mum's got hold of some bunting," said Charly.

"Excellent!" said Meg. "Now all we've got to do is wait for the newspaper to come out tomorrow."

"Yes," agreed Flo. "Let's hope people write in with their stories."

★ ♥ ★ ♥ ★ ♥ ★

The Glitter Girls didn't have to wait long. Only a few days later, the newspaper office delivered a big bag of responses from readers to the school office.

"Come on – let's have a look in the bag!" Hannah urged, as soon as they got back to her house after school.

"Yes, let's look," cried Flo excitedly, diving into the bag and handing around letters and pictures to each of her friends.

There was silence for a while as everyone read the tributes and memories people had sent in for Grace. Finally Zoe broke the tranquillity.

"Wow – all these people really love Grace," she said.

The others agreed.

"And look at all of these cards and letters – one person has even sent in a school report that Grace wrote about him!"

"And there's all these pictures too!" said Flo.

"I've got at least twelve things here," Charly said.

"How many are there altogether?" asked Meg.

The Glitter Girls counted the piles – there were nearly fifty!

"Fantastic!" Meg said, putting all the photographs, cards and letters together. "That will help us to make Grace's project book truly special."

"Girls?" It was Mrs Giles calling up the stairs. "Teatime!"

And the Glitter Girls were off!

★ ♥ ★ ♥ ★ ♥ ★

As the Glitter Girls tucked into their tea they updated Mrs Giles on all the preparations for Grace's party.

"So how are you going to write up this book of yours?" Mrs Giles asked.

"Well we thought we'd try to write a story of Grace's life, starting from when she was at school," explained Meg.

"And we're going to paste in the stories about Grace that people are writing for us so that they fit in between the bits we are going to write about Grace," said Flo.

"And we've chosen some pictures, which my dad's helping to get copied," added Meg.

"And I'm going to do a wall display, too," explained Flo. "Kim's going to help me."

"That all sounds terrific," Mrs Giles said. "I've been thinking about this patchwork quilt as well."

"We haven't got that much time left, have we?" said Hannah.

"No," agreed Mrs Giles. "But I was just thinking that you could put together a patchwork quilt showing all the things that Grace has done for the town."

"How could we do that?" Zoe wondered.

"Well, I'd help you of course," explained Mrs Giles. "But I thought we could make some simple templates – you know, the school, the evacuees, all the societies that Grace has worked for like the Brownies and stuff, and make a square for each one."

"It sounds like a brilliant idea, Mrs Giles," said Meg. "But do you really think we could get it done in time?"

"Well each of you could work on a square – and I'm sure that your mums and maybe your dads could help too," suggested Mrs Giles.

"Let's see if we can do it!" urged Flo.

"Yes let's!" said Charly.

"OK," said Mrs Giles, smiling. "I'll draw up a pattern and start cutting it out. Perhaps we can start on it at the weekend."

"Brilliant!" said Zoe.

"It'll be fantastic!" agreed Meg. "Grace will love it!"

Just as the girls were sharing their excitement the phone rang and Mrs Giles picked it up. Hannah, Meg, Flo, Zoe and Charly could see from her face that it wasn't good news. As soon as she put down the receiver, Hannah said, "What's up, Mum?"

"Oh girls . . . I'm so sorry. . ." Mrs Giles sat down on her chair at the kitchen table and stared at the Glitter Girls.

"What is it, Mrs Giles?" Flo asked.

"It's Grace, I'm afraid," Mrs Giles replied. "That was your mum, Zoe, ringing from the hospital. She's just seen Grace there. She's had a fall and been taken to hospital!"

Chapter 8

"Is Grace going to be all right?" Meg was asking the question that the other Glitter Girls wanted to know but didn't dare ask.

"I don't know, Meg," Mrs Giles answered truthfully.

"What happened though?" Charly wanted to know.

"I think that Grace was trying to get up from her chair when she lost her balance and fell. Mrs Billingham found her and an ambulance took her to hospital. That's how your mum knows, Zoe. Apparently she was on duty when Grace arrived in Accident and Emergency."

"So Grace is in hospital?" Zoe asked.

"Yes – your mum is going to ring again

in a while to tell us how she is," Mrs Giles explained.

"Is Grace going to die?" Hannah whispered.

"We don't really know what's happened to her yet," said Mrs Giles, putting a comforting arm around her daughter. "But we must remember that Grace is a very old lady."

The Glitter Girls looked at each other in complete silence. Grace just couldn't die! She couldn't!

"Now come on girls," said Mrs Giles. "Let's try and keep cheerful."

The Glitter Girls didn't feel much like talking – they were too worried about Grace. They sat in almost total silence and it seemed like hours before the phone rang again.

It was Zoe's mum, and Mrs Giles immediately passed the phone over to Zoe.

"Mum! How's Grace? Have you seen her?"

The Glitter Girls gathered round Zoe as she spoke to her mum. "What did she say?" Meg asked, as soon as Zoe put the phone back on the receiver.

"She says she's got a nasty bruise on her face," explained Zoe. "And they've taken her to have an X-ray in case she's broken her arm. Apparently it's really sore."

"Oh, poor Grace!" sighed Flo.

"Can we go and see her?" said Charly.

"I don't think that would be a good idea today girls," said Mrs Giles. "I should think that she probably needs lots of rest."

"Do you think Grace will be well enough to have her party still?" Hannah asked.

"Let's hope so," said her mum kindly. "But in the meantime, I think you girls ought to get on with your project, don't you? Then you can make sure that Grace has the best birthday ever."

Despite being so worried about Grace, the Glitter Girls were determined to get on with their party plans. At school the next day, they asked Miss Stanley if they could write to the Queen on school notepaper.

"I think that sounds like a great idea, girls," Miss Stanley grinned. "I'll get you some paper at lunchtime. Now, tell me, how are all your other plans going for the party?"

Between them, the Glitter Girls told Miss Stanley all about the plans they had and the things they were finding out about the town and Grace's life there. They also told Miss Stanley about Grace's accident.

"But we want to make sure everything's ready for the party," explained Hannah.

"Yes," said Flo. "So if Grace does come out of hospital in time for her birthday, we can make sure she has a great welcome home."

"Well, I think you are quite right to carry on girls," Miss Stanley said. "I think your project sounds like the best get well card anyone could have."

"Yes," said Charly sadly. "But will Grace be well enough to come to her own party?"

"We'll have to hope very hard that she will!" said Meg, determined as ever.

★ ♥ ★ ♥ ★ ♥ ★

That afternoon, the Glitter Girls met up at Flo's house. Charly, Meg, Hannah, Zoe and Flo sat round as Flo carefully wrote out the letter to the Queen asking her to send Grace a telegram for her birthday. They made sure to mention that Grace had been ill.

"Great," said Meg, as she folded the letter and placed it in an envelope. "We can post this tomorrow morning on the way to school."

"Now," said Flo, "let me show you how I've been thinking about doing the wall display."

"Great," said Zoe and Hannah.

Flo took out her sketchpad and displayed it in

front of the others. They could see neat diagrams showing the basis for a great display.

"It's going to be a real celebration of Grace's life, isn't it?" said Charly.

"I really like the way you've done it as a time-line," said Meg.

"Well, it seemed the best way. You know, Grace's book will have the more personal things about her in it and I thought the time-line could show Grace growing up in the town and all the changes that have happened over the last century." Flo popped her thumb in her mouth as she sat thoughtfully looking at her ideas.

"Perfect!" said Hannah. "Especially with all those photographs Meg's dad is copying from the Town Hall."

"You lot can help me with the banner over the weekend," said Flo.

"Course," the others replied.

"Now all we've got to do is go to the newspaper office and see if there are any more letters for Grace," said Meg.

"I expect there will be," Charly said with certainty.

"Especially after they did that extra bit in the last issue about Grace being in hospital."

"Well, let's go and see as soon as we can," said Zoe.

Chapter 9

Charly was right! There *was* another pile of cards, photographs and letters waiting for them at the newspaper office. Over the next few days, the Glitter Girls spent their spare moments carefully putting the many stories they had received from people in order.

"We can't put them into the book just yet though," said Meg sensibly. "After all, we've got two weeks to go before the party and we don't know how many more stories we're going to get."

"I think we should put them in a ring binder," suggested Flo. "That way we can move things about more easily."

"Good idea," said Charly.

"How's your dad getting on with the pictures Meg?" asked Hannah.

"He's collected them from the Town Hall and he's going to sort the copies out over the weekend."

"Good," said Flo. "Then I can get started on the wall display with Kim."

"And my mum says that we can go and see Grace on Saturday!" said Charly.

"Go Glitter!" they all said happily.

It was Friday night and Hannah and her mum were busily laying scraps of fabric out on her mum's workroom table. Mrs Giles had the most brilliant workroom which was filled with fantastic fabrics and gossamer sewing silks. The Glitter Girls loved every chance they had to explore all the wonderful treasures there.

RAT-tat-tat! There was a knock at the workroom door.

"Who is it?" Hannah whispered as her mum carried on sorting things on the table.

"GG!" came the reply.

Hannah quickly opened the door to find the four other Glitter Girls all standing there with their mums. They'd come to help make the quilt for Grace.

"Hi!" everyone said at once.

"How is Grace?" Mrs Giles asked Dr Baker as she sat down on one of the stools surrounding the work table.

"Well, she's still very badly bruised," explained Zoe's mum. "But she is just so cheerful and determined not to let the accident make her depressed. And she's really looking forward to the visit from the Glitter Girls tomorrow!" she added.

"So are we!" said Meg.

"Well, girls," said Mrs Giles. "If we're going to get this patchwork quilt sorted, we'd better get on with it!"

Hannah's mum showed everyone the design that she'd come up with. There were squares for the Brownies and Scouts, the school, the Community Hall that they'd also discovered Grace had helped to get built, the Town Band – and more. Just about everything that had happened in the town seemed to have something to do with Grace!

"Now, I've put the squares and the fabric in position at the table," explained Mrs Giles. "I've put names on the squares so if you can all find your places – it'll be a bit of a squeeze, I'm afraid – you can get started."

"And finished!" laughed Mrs Eng, Flo's mum. "Then we can go back to our house for supper! Flo's dad has made us one of his special Chinese meals."

"Go Glitter!" all the girls said.

"Go Glitter!" the mums called back, their hands held above their heads, just like the Glitter Girls! Everyone laughed. The sewing had begun!

★ ♥ ★ ♥ ★ ♥ ★

On Saturday morning, the Glitter Girls met up at Meg's house.

"Wasn't it good last night?" Charly said.

"Yes – the quilt looks great, doesn't it?" said Hannah, proud of her mum's talents.

"Your mum's so good at that sort of stuff, isn't she?" said Flo.

"Your dad's not bad at cooking either!" Meg said.

"Girls?" Meg's mum called up the stairs. "Meg's dad's here to take you to the hospital!"

The Glitter Girls raced down the stairs and out on to the drive.

"Hello girls!" Meg's dad said cheerfully, as they bundled into the car. "Shall we go?"

"Go Glitter!" they all replied enthusiastically.

The Glitter Girls were really excited at the thought of seeing Grace again. It had been nearly a week since she'd had her fall and Dr

Baker, who'd popped in to see her, said she was still fragile but a lot better.

During the journey, the Glitter Girls were delighted to hear that Meg's dad had brought the pictures and photographs that he had copied with him.

"Great, that means I can start the wall display with Kim tomorrow!" Flo said, as they arrived at the hospital.

The Glitter Girls quickly made their way to Grace's ward, and announced their arrival to the nurse at the main desk.

"She's been expecting you!" said the nurse, smiling. "She's in the second bed on the left."

"I'll pop and have a coffee in the canteen," said Meg's dad, heading for the door. "See you later!"

"See you, Dad," Meg whispered. Then she and the girls swiftly and quietly made their way to Grace's bedside.

"Hello Grace," they all said quietly.

"Well hello, Glitter Girls," Grace smiled back. They could see a nasty yellow and black bruise on Grace's face and her arm was in a sling, but her smile was welcoming. "It's lovely to see you all. My, don't you look smart – all in the same jackets!"

The Glitter Girls were very proud of their jackets and were pleased that Grace liked them too.

"And don't you all look lovely with all those braids and ribbons in your hair?" Grace said, admiring each of the Glitter Girls in turn.

"We've brought you some flowers," Flo explained, placing them on the table next to Grace's bed.

"Thank you, girls," said Grace.

"Are you feeling any better?" Hannah asked.

"Much, thank you," Grace smiled. "I'm still a little tired. But then I am nearly a hundred! I've done lots of things in my time so I probably should feel tired by now!"

Grace laughed gently and the Glitter Girls did too. They smiled conspiratorially at each other. They knew better than a lot of people exactly how much Grace had done in her life! But they didn't want to tell Grace that.

"Oh – and do you know?" said Grace. "I think I'm going to be allowed to go back to The Beeches on Monday!"

"That's great, Grace!" said Charly.

"I think it calls for one of your 'Go Glitters!'" said Grace, waving the arm that wasn't in a sling in the air.

"Go Glitter!" the girls replied.

Chapter 10

On Sunday afternoon, Charly, Zoe, Hannah and Meg went to visit Flo. She was busy with her sister, setting up the wall display in their garage. Even though the garage door was open, the four girls gave the usual Glitter Girl knock – RAT-tat-tat!

"GG!" replied Flo, as her friends stepped inside the garage.

Flo and Kim had already pieced the backing boards together and were busy trying to work out the order of the pictures and photos.

"Hey, they look great, don't they?" said Charly.

"Yes, Dad said he thought we'd chosen some really good pictures," agreed Meg.

"Grace is just going to love all these, isn't she?" sighed Hannah.

"I hope so," said Kim.

"We're putting some to one side," explained Flo. "So that they can go in Grace's special book."

The Glitter Girls were hoping to finish Grace's book that week. Between them, they had worked out what they each wanted to write about the different things that Grace had been involved with. And on Monday afternoon, they had arranged to go and see the mayoress to talk about the final preparations for the party which was set for the 24th, Grace's birthday.

"Tell us what to do then, and we'll help," said Zoe.

"OK," said Flo. "I need some of you to use this special card to mount the pictures on."

"I'll do that!" said Hannah and Zoe at the same time.

They giggled. "Looks like we've got the job,"

smiled Zoe, and she and Hannah got to work carefully gluing the photos down.

"What can Charly and I do?" Meg asked.

"Well, Kim and I have pencilled all the headings and the time links for the display," Flo explained. "Can you two felt pen neatly over them?"

"Perfect!" said Charly.

"Just give us the pens," smiled Meg, "and we'll get going."

And the Glitter Girls spent the rest of the afternoon happily making the display.

★　♥　★　♥　★　♥　★

On Monday, the girls went with Charly's mum to the Town Hall. Mrs Kirk was waiting for them in her office.

"Come in girls," she smiled. "Now, how are you getting on with your book?"

"Well, we've done everything we can so far. We've just got the last few stories to fit in," Zoe said.

"And have you decided how you are going to present it to her?" Mrs Kirk asked.

"Well, we thought we'd wrap it up and give it to her," suggested Hannah. "Along with the quilt."

"I must say I can't wait to see the quilt," Mrs Kirk said. "But why don't we do something different with the book?" She smiled – she clearly had something special in mind already!

"Like what?" Flo asked.

Mrs Kirk explained that she thought it would be lovely if Grace arrived at the Town Hall, only thinking that she had come to have a quiet cup of tea with the mayoress. But then she could be taken into the main hall where everyone would be hiding quietly – then the party could begin!

"And, you see, I thought it would be lovely for everyone there to be told by you girls about everything that Grace has done for the town and its people over the last one hundred years. There's so much that's she's done, that I don't think anyone else can realize just how much. Unless you tell them!"

"That's a brilliant idea!" said Meg, frantically writing everything down in her book.

"So will you all take turns in narrating Grace's life story?" Mrs Kirk asked the Glitter Girls.

"Go Glitter!" they confirmed!

The week passed in a flurry of activity. In-between their other activities, after school and homework, the Glitter Girls got together as often as they could for their special meetings when they planned who would tell which bit of Grace's story. Meg kept a meticulous list of who would speak and when. On Wednesday after-noon, Mrs Wadhurst asked to see the Glitter Girls.

"Hello girls," she said smiling. "I've got this for you!"

She was holding up an envelope that didn't

have a stamp on it. Instead it had a special crest and was handwritten. Immediately, the Glitter Girls realized it was a reply from Buckingham Palace! Quickly they opened it. It wasn't from the Queen herself but from one of her staff, telling them that the Queen would be delighted to send Grace a telegram for her hundredth birthday. It was going to be sent to the mayoress to present to Grace! Now the party would be perfect!

★ ♥ ★ ♥ ★ ♥ ★

That afternoon after school, the Glitter Girls went to visit Grace at The Beeches. They were delighted to see that, even though she still had her arm in a sling, Grace was feeling much better. Excitedly, Grace told them all about how she was going to have tea with the mayoress on her birthday. The Glitter Girls were bursting with the brilliant surprise that they had for Grace – but they didn't want to spoil everything they had worked so hard for.

"And Charly's kind mother is going to do my hair for me," Grace said to the girls.

"We'll do our best to come and visit you on the day," said Meg. "But it will probably be difficult because of school and stuff."

"Of course!" said Grace. "I quite understand – but it would be lovely to see you if you have a chance!"

Little did Grace know!

★ ♥ ★ ♥ ★ ♥ ★

On Thursday, the Glitter Girls went to Charly's house after school to make Grace's birthday cake.

"I thought we'd make her a sponge and put butter icing on it," suggested Mrs Fisher.

After washing their hands and donning their aprons, Hannah, Charly, Meg, Flo and Zoe had a great time mixing, baking and spreading. Hannah and Charly took it in turns to mix up all the ingredients after helping Mrs Fisher to measure them out. Then Meg beat the butter icing while Flo and Zoe sorted the frosted icing that was going to go on the top.

Because this was an extra-special celebration for Grace, they all decided the cake had to be iced in true Glitter Girl pink. They would spell out a special message for Grace on top of the cake using silver sugar balls and chocolate icing.

"Hey," said Zoe, sniffing the air in the busy kitchen as the cake was baking. "Doesn't that smell just great?"

"Mmm!" the others agreed and then got on with the delicious business of licking and scraping the mixing bowls while the cake baked.

"Time for the icing!" said Mrs Fisher when the baked cake had cooled.

The Girls smoothed the pink frosting over the top and sides of the cake, and Flo got ready to pipe some writing.

"What shall I write?" Flo asked.

"'Happy 100th Birthday Grace' sounds cool to me!" said Hannah, and the others agreed with her.

"I want to eat it now!" said Charly, when it was finished.

"Me too!" agreed Flo and Zoe.

"Well – why don't I put it in a cake tin, and keep it safe until the party?" laughed Mrs Fisher.

Reluctantly they agreed.

★ ♥ ★ ♥ ★ ♥ ★

It was the 24th at last! Mrs Wadhurst had decided that Grace's birthday was such a special occasion that she said that everyone in the Glitter Girls' class should go to the party!

Straight after lunch, the Glitter Girls changed into their jackets and favourite pink and shimmery outfits that they so loved wearing, ready to set off with their class to the Town Hall so that they could help with the decorations.

Before they left, the Glitter Girls proudly went to show Miss Stanley Grace's book.

"This is wonderful, girls," Miss Stanley smiled. "A special project and a very special gift for Mrs Greenfield too. Now keep it safe until we get there."

Just as they were leaving, Meg went through the checklist that she had prepared. "Wall display?"

"Here!" said Flo, who was carrying it with Charly.

"Quilt?"

"Here!" said Hannah.

"Book? Oh, I've got that! Badge?"

"Got it!" said Zoe. The Glitter Girls had made Grace an honorary member of the Glitter Girls so they had made her one of their special badges!

"Let's go then!"

The party was soon to begin!

★ ♥ ★ ♥ ★ ♥ ★

With everyone helping out, the hall was soon decorated and ready for Grace. There were balloons and streamers all around the walls and the Glitter Girls had positioned their time-line display carefully along the main wall. Just as they finished, people started busily arriving and making their way to the main hall. There were lots of people there, but everyone was trying to be as quiet as they possibly could! After all, they didn't want to spoil Grace's surprise.

"Hello girls," Mrs Kirk said when she saw them. "I've got the telegram! And the band is here! Do you have everything you need?"

"I think so," Meg replied, butterflies in her stomach. She so wanted Grace's party to be brilliant!

"Well, Grace will be here shortly, so I'd better go downstairs!"

About fifteen minutes later, with everyone in the hall struggling to be very quiet, the receptionist came in and whispered that Grace was on her way! Moments later, the door creaked open and Grace and Mrs Kirk walked slowly into the room. Immediately, everyone started to sing "Happy Birthday" to Grace!

Grace was stunned. She was being supported by Mrs Kirk as she walked but at the sound of the singing, she stopped still and just looked around at everyone with amazement.

As everyone burst into applause, someone found a chair for Grace to sit in and, after she had carefully sat down with Mrs Kirk's help, she put her good hand to her mouth, still stunned. Then, as silence fell, Grace quietly said, "Thank you . . . thank you so much . . . thank you all. . ."

The Glitter Girls thought they could see tears in Grace's eyes and suddenly worried that maybe the party was too much for her after her accident. But then Grace smiled and gently laughed and said, "Oh thank you! I think this is the best birthday I've had in a hundred years!"

★ ♥ ★ ♥ ★ ♥ ★

Grace gazed around the room smiling at everyone and she spotted the Glitter Girls straight away!

"Did you girls know about this?" Grace asked.

"Just a bit!" said Mrs Kirk. "In fact, you have these girls to thank for getting us all organized to be here today! Now," Mrs Kirk turned to the Glitter Girls, "I think you've got an important story to tell everyone, haven't you?"

The Glitter Girls smiled and came forward. The room fell silent again as Charly started to read:

"Grace Greenfield was born in this town exactly one hundred years ago today. And this is the story of her fantastic life and her dedication to our town. . ."

One by one, the Glitter Girls unfolded Grace's special story. And when it was over, Hannah said, "And this is a special memento of your work for our town from all of us." She handed over the quilt and gave Grace a kiss on the cheek.

"Well, thank you so much girls. Thank you to everyone!" Grace started to thumb gently through her book, which Meg had placed on a table next to her.

Zoe stepped forward and pinned the special Glitter Girl badge to Grace's dress and then everyone cheered and watched as the mayoress presented Grace with the Queen's telegram. Then everyone sang "Happy Birthday" all over again!

It was a great party and people stood for ages, queueing up to speak to Grace and looking at the Glitter Girls' time-line while they waited. There were people she'd taught, evacuees who had had a temporary home in the town during the Second World War, ladies from the Townswomen's Guild – some of them hadn't seen Grace for years but word had spread that Grace was having a surprise party and they'd come back especially.

But after a while, Grace was beginning to look tired and Mrs Kirk offered to take her home in the mayoress's special car!

"Thank you for such a marvellous party, Glitter Girls!" said Grace as she left the hall.

"We loved it, Grace!" the Glitter Girls replied. "And thank you for everything you've done for the town and our school!"

"Go Glitter!" Grace grinned.

"Go Glitter!" replied Charly, Zoe, Hannah, Meg and Flo.

As everyone gathered outside to wave Grace

off, Mrs Kirk called everyone to a hush.

"I forgot to tell everyone that the Town Council has made an important decision about the new Community Room at the back of the Town Hall. We've decided that, in recognition and honour of all her hard work, we're going to call the room the Grace Greenfield Room."

Everyone made a deafening cheer! The Glitter Girls looked at each other and smiled and hugged.

"This has been one of our best projects ever!" said Flo.

"Go Glitter!" her friends cried in response!